First published by Parragon in 2013
Parragon
Chartist House
15–17 Trim Street
Bath BA1 1HA, UK
www.parragon.com

Written by David Bedford
Illustrated by Brenna Vaughan and Henry St Leger
Edited by Laura Baker
Designed by Ailsa Cullen
Production by Rob Simenton

ISBN 978-1-4723-0298-4
Printed in China

I love my Mummy

PaRragon

Bath · New York · Singapore · Hong Kong · Cologne · Delhi
Melbourne · Amsterdam · Johannesburg · Shenzhen

One morning, Little Deer didn't want to
play in his garden any more.
"I want to see new things,"
he told his mummy.
"Then let's go exploring," said Mummy Deer,
"and see what new things we can find."

"This way!" said Little Deer excitedly,
and he hurried ahead, while Mummy followed
behind, watching over him.

Little Deer **hopped** along the grass by the hanging willow tree. Then he slowly crossed the wobbly stones, watching the stream as it trickled gently beside him.

"Don't get your feet wet," warned Mummy.

"I won't!" said Little Deer, as he

wiggled
and
wobbled.

Little Deer counted red and orange butterflies, then squeezed through thick, tangly bushes.

"Don't get stuck,"
warned Mummy.

"I won't!" called Little Deer, as he
skipped out the other side.
"Hurry up, Mummy!"
he called. "There's lots more to see."

"Look!" said Little Deer.
"A hill that goes up to the clouds!"

"Is it too high?" said his mummy.

"It's not too high for me," said Little Deer, panting as he climbed step by step all the way to the top.

"I can see forever!"
cried Little Deer, standing tall
on his tiptoes.

His mummy stood close beside
him, but Little Deer was
beginning to wobble again,

and suddenly...

"Wheeee!"

cried Little Deer as he
skidded and slid, landing
with a swoosh in a pile of
fallen leaves.

"Are you okay, Little Deer?"
asked his mummy.

"Yes!" giggled Little Deer. "I am!"

Little Deer sat in the meadow with his mummy, watching the bees buzzing in the warm sun.

Suddenly, Little Deer sat up. "Mummy?" he said. "Which way is home?" He looked all around him.

"I'm lost!"

Mummy Deer nuzzled Little Deer's nose. "We'll soon find our way back," she said soothingly. "We just have to remember how we got here."

Little Deer thought and thought. At last, he began to remember…

"We came over the hill!"
cried Little Deer, and he
scampered back to the hill that
went up to the clouds.

Mummy Deer helped him climb
quickly to the top, where...

"Yippee!"

cried Little Deer. "I can see the way from here!"

Little Deer and his mummy skidded down the other side of the hill to find what came next.

"We squeezed through the tangly bushes!" Little Deer told his mummy, and he scurried back through the hole he'd made, with his little tail wagging. Mummy Deer gave him a helping nudge.

"Which way now?" said Little Deer's
mummy, when they were on the other side.
Little Deer saw the red and orange butterflies, and
heard the tinkling sound of a stream...

"The wobbly stones!" cheered
Little Deer, as he hurried across the stream.

"Don't get your feet wet, Mummy," he warned.

"I won't!" laughed Mummy Deer. **"But who's going to be home first?"**

Little Deer knew the way
from here.

He ran as fast as his little
legs would take him,
along the grass by the
willowy tree until…

"I'm home first!"

said Little Deer, and he jumped and jumped all around his little garden.

Little Deer flopped
down in the sunshine
beside Mummy.

"I love exploring," said Little Deer happily.

"And I love
my mummy!"